Ferry Tail

Written by **Katharine Kenah**

Illustrated by **Nicole Wong**

For my sister Mackie, and the real Walter, with love.

KK

For Fran.

NW

Sleeping Bear Press

315 E. Eisenhower Parkway, Ste. 200
Ann Arbor, MI 48108
www.sleepingbearpress.com

Printed and bound in the United States.

10 9 8 7 6 5 4 3 2 1

Library of Congress Cataloging-in-Publication Data

Kenah, Katharine.
Ferry tail / written by Katharine Kenah ; illustrated by Nicole Wong
pages cm
Summary: "Fed up with Cupcake the cat, Walter the dog leaves
his ferryboat home. Unwanted and unfamiliar with his island
surroundings, Walter relies on none other than Cupcake to guide
him home"— Provided by publisher
ISBN 978-1-58536-829-7
[1. Dogs—Fiction. 2. Cats—Fiction. 3. Ferries—Fiction.]
I. Wong, Nicole (Nicole E.), illustrator. II. Title.
PZ7.K315Fer 2014
[E]—dc23
2013024887

Walter was a ferry dog.

When cars came on board for the morning run, Walter was there to greet them.

He barked at seagulls,

posed in family pictures,
and kept an eye on babies.

Being the ferry dog
was a big job, but
Walter *loved* it.

He had work to do everywhere.

The Captain needed his help. Walter brought him the newspaper every morning. "Thank you, Walter," said the Captain. "You are one fine dog."

The Engineer needed his help. "Do you think this boat is ready to go?" she asked. When Walter wagged his tail, they sat down together and listened to the engines roar.

The Cook needed his help. "Come here, Walter," he called. "Taste this bacon for me." Walter hurried right over and gobbled it up. "Breakfast is ready!" announced the Cook.

Walter loved everyone and everything on the ferry ... *except* the Captain's cat.

Cupcake wore a collar with jewels. Cupcake slept in a fluffy round bed in the Captain's cabin. Walter slept on blankets in a cozy corner of the car deck.

Cupcake played with a toy mouse that squeaked. She carried it everywhere. Whenever Walter got near Cupcake, she dropped her squeaky mouse and poked him with her paws.

One gray day the weather matched Walter's mood. He was tired of rough waves and rainy decks. The passengers were staying inside to keep warm. They were talking, reading, working, and eating. No one seemed to need his help.

Cupcake made his day even worse.
She tasted bacon for the Cook.

She sat with the Engineer
while the engines roared.

When Walter brought the Captain the newspaper, Cupcake shredded the front page.
The Captain saw the mess, looked at Walter and said, "Bad dog."

Walter decided it was time to leave the ferry! He ran down
to the car deck and waited. The moment the ferry tied
up at the dock, Walter dashed over the ramp
and onto the island.

The ground felt strange under his feet. It always did at first. The island didn't roll like the ferry. It wasn't hard like the deck. It was soft and sandy and seemed bigger than the ocean. There was land everywhere! Walter ran and ran and *ran*.

He came to a town. Scooters
and buses whooshed past him.

Fire engines blared
their horns.

Children on swings moved
up and down like they were
riding waves without water!

Things on land were fast and loud and strange.

Then Walter saw a truck delivering newspapers. He knew about newspapers!
He picked up the newspapers and carried them back to the truck.

"Go away, dog!" yelled the driver.

He saw people lined up at a hot dog stand.
Walter got in line.

"Go away, dog!" called the customers.

Walter walked and walked. Soon he was tired and hungry.
When Walter sat down to rest on a grassy bank, he saw a
big family nearby. They were taking pictures!

He rushed over to help. Walter posed in front of the
cameras and kept an eye on the babies.

"Go away, dog!" said the mothers and fathers, sisters and brothers, cousins and uncles and aunts. The babies didn't say anything.

Walter kept moving. When he tried
to greet cars, they honked at him.

Ribbons of fog floated in the air. The day was getting darker. Walter was getting chilly. He missed the ferry … and he had no idea where it was!

Walter *had* to find the ferry before it was too late. What if it left the island without him? He ran in circles. He ran in straight lines. It was no use. He couldn't see anything. The fog was like a white blanket around him.

Walter sat down and felt miserable. Who would bring newspapers to the Captain? Who would tell the Engineer when the ferry was ready to go? Who would taste food for the Cook?

Suddenly Walter heard a squeak and felt a poke. He whirled around and saw Cupcake! She was sitting behind him, holding her toy mouse.

When she reached out a paw to poke him again, Walter poked Cupcake... *twice*.

She turned and ran back to the ferry. Walter chased her the whole way.

"Welcome back," said the Cook. "We were worried about you. Are you hungry?"

"We were worried about *both* of you," said the Captain. He picked
up Cupcake and patted Walter. "You are one fine dog," he said.

The Engineer asked, "Do you think this
boat is ready to go?" Walter wagged
his tail and they sat down together,
listening to the engines roar.

When cars came on board for the morning run, Walter was there
to greet them. He barked at seagulls, posed in family pictures,
and kept an eye on babies. Sometimes Cupcake came, too.

Walter was a ferry dog. The
ferry couldn't run without him.

FEB — 2014